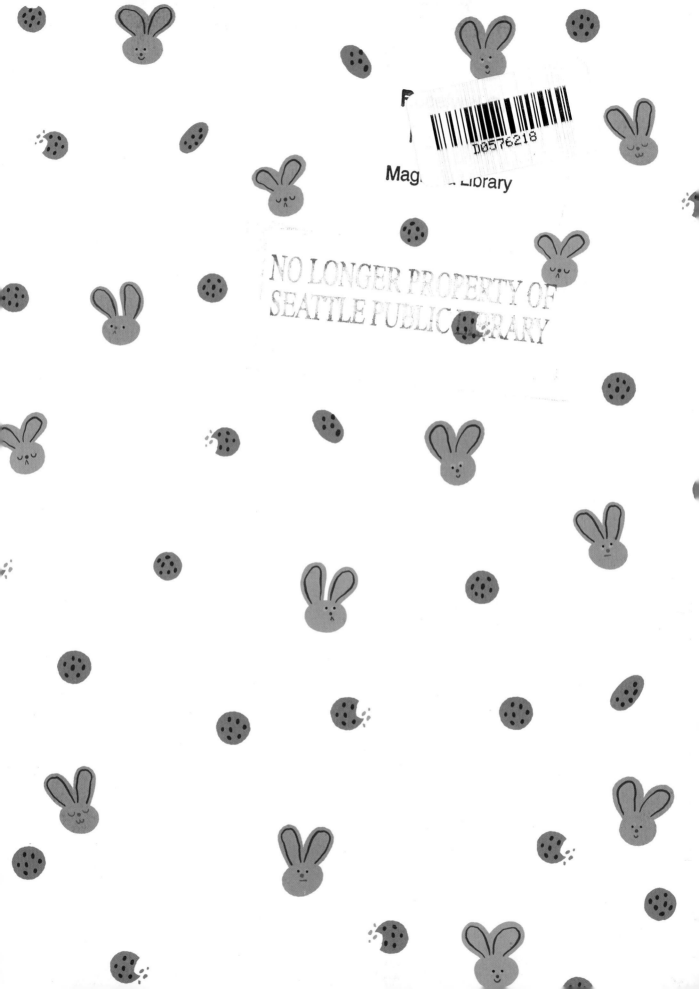

Mag... Library

NO LONGER PROPERTY OF
SEATTLE PUBLIC LIBRARY

MY BEST FRIEND, SOMETIMES

WRITTEN BY NAOMI DANIS   ILLUSTRATED BY CINTA ARRIBAS

POW!

BROOKYN, NY

ONE DAY AT LUNCH
  I SAT NEXT TO STEPHANIE.

"IF YOU GIVE ME A COOKIE," SHE SAID TO ME,
"I'LL BE YOUR BEST FRIEND."

I GAVE HER A COOKIE. IT WAS CHOCOLATE CHIP.

STEPHANIE AND ME. WHAT DO WE LIKE TO DO?

SIT NEXT TO EACH OTHER.

TALK.

NOTICE WHO GOT A HAIRCUT.

OR WHO HAS A CREAM CHEESE AND PICKLE SANDWICH.

GIGGLE. WHISPER.

RUN AT RECESS.

PLAY PRETEND.

"PRETEND I'M THE MOTHER AND YOU'RE THE BABY."

"PRETEND I'M THE DOCTOR AND YOU NEED A SHOT."

OR: "PRETEND WE'RE GETTING MARRIED."

WE TELL EACH OTHER SECRETS
OTHER PEOPLE MIGHT
NOT BELIEVE.

WHEN I GROW UP I AM GOING
TO LIVE ON THE MOON.

STEPHANIE IS GOING TO
HAVE A HUNDRED BABIES.

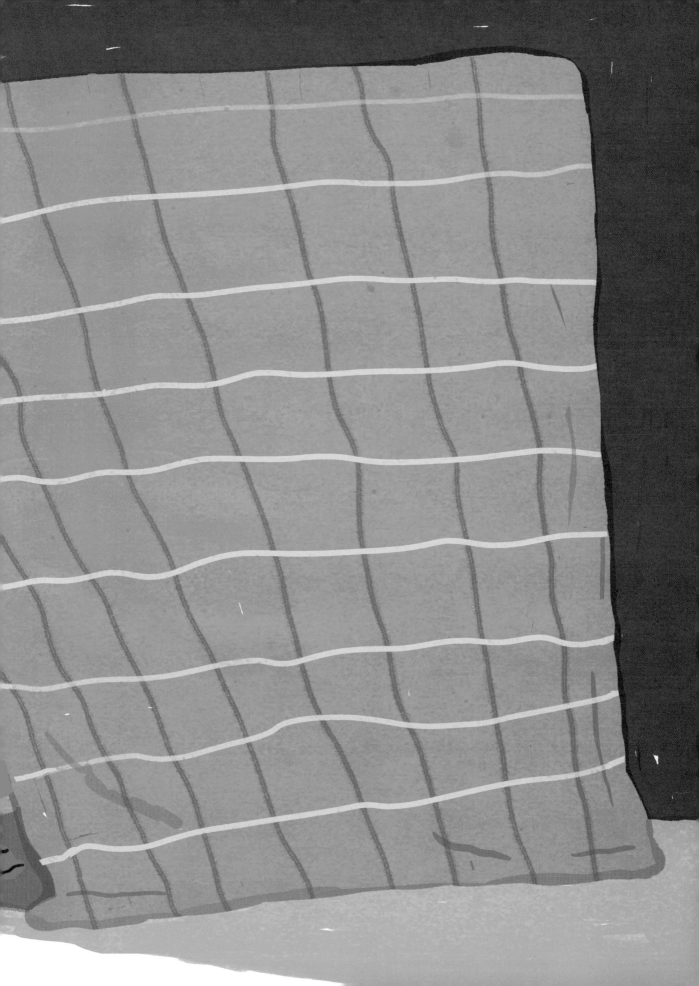

STEPHANIE AND I LIKE EACH OTHER.
AND WE DON'T LIKE EACH OTHER.
BOTH.

THINGS DON'T ALWAYS GO THE WAY I WANT.
BECAUSE WE DON'T ALWAYS LIKE THE SAME THINGS.

WHEN i WANT TO RACE ACROSS THE PLAYGROUN AT RECESS,
STEPHANiE WANTS TO SiNG A CLAPPiNG SONG.

I GET NEW SHOES AND STEPHANIE DOESN'T TELL ME SHE LIKES THEM. MY MOM SAYS I SHOULD BE GLAD THAT I LIKE MY SHOES AND STEPHANIE LIKES HER SHOES.

IT'S NOT IMPORTANT, MY MOM SAYS, FOR STEPHANIE TO LIKE MY SHOES. BUT STILL, I WISH SHE WOULD, AND I WISH SHE WOULD TELL ME.

OR SOMETIMES STEPHANIE AND I WANT THE EXACT SAME THING AND WE CAN'T BOTH HAVE IT AT THE EXACT SAME TIME.

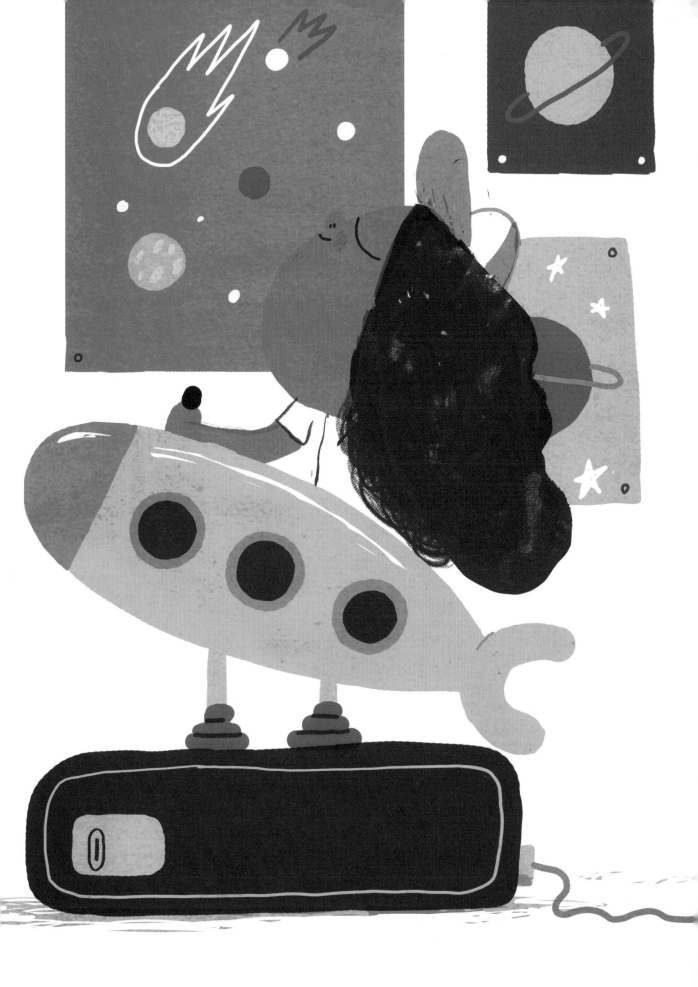

STEPHANIE BRINGS MY FAVORITE CANDY TO SCHOOL AND DOESN'T SAVE A PIECE FOR ME, EVEN THROUGH SHE KNOWS I LIKE IT BECAUSE I ALWAYS ASK HER FOR SOME.

"SORRY," SHE SAYS. "TODAY I JUST FEEL LIKE EATING IT ALL UP MYSELF."
WELL, AT LEAST SHE SAID SORRY.

WHEN I HAVE A COLD, I STAY HOME FROM SCHOOL.
I WORRY STEPHANIE MIGHT FIND A NEW BEST FRIEND,
SOMEONE ELSE TO GIVE HER A COOKIE AT LUNCH.

"HI," I SAY. "HI," SHE SAYS.
"WE MISSED YOU IN SCHOOL TODAY. I HOPE YOU FEEL BETTER SOON."
I FEEL BETTER ALREADY BECAUSE SHE CALLED.

ONE DAY STEPHANIE IS MAD AT ME, SO MAD
THAT SHE ISN'T TALKING TO ME.

BUT BECAUSE WE ARE BEST FRIENDS, SHE SITS
NEXT TO ME ON THE SCHOOL BUS ANYWAY, NOT
TALKING TO ME ALL THE BUMPY WAY HOME.

I CAN'T EVEN REMEMBER WHAT HER MAD IS ABOUT. IS SHE MAD BECAUSE IT WILL BE MY TURN TO TAKE THE GUINEA PIG HOME THIS WEEKEND AND SHE WANTS IT TO BE HER TURN?

I DON'T KNOW. SHE WON'T TELL ME.
I FEEL SAD. AND CONFUSED.

EVEN THOUGH IT FEELS LIKE WE ARE BETTER
AT BEING ENEMIES, I HOPE WE CAN GO BACK TO FEELING LIKE FRIENDS.

FINALLY WE GET TO MY STOP.
 I LEAN OVER AND WHISPER, "SEE YOU TOMORROW."

AS THE BUS PULLS AWAY i LOOK UP
AT THE WiNDOW WHERE SHE iS SiTTiNG.
STEPHANiE iS STARiNG AT ME.

SUDDENLY SHE SMILES AT ME.
i SMILE BACK. i FEEL HAPPY AGAIN.

MAYBE A SMILE IS EVEN BETTER THAN A COOKIE.

For Madelyn, it's true, in here is some of you. —N.D.

To my mother, Maite, who taught me the pleasure of drawing. —C.A.

Text © 2020 by Naomi Danis
Illustrations © 2020 by Cinta Arribas

All rights reserved. No part of this book may be reproduced in any manner in any media, or transmitted by any means whatsoever, electronic or mechanical (including photocopy, film or video recording, Internet posting, or any other information storage and retrieval system), without the prior written permission of the publisher.

Published by POW! a division of powerHouse Packaging & Supply, Inc.
32 Adams Street, Brooklyn, NY 11201-1021

info@powkidsbooks.com

www.powkidsbooks.com

www.powerHouseBooks.com

www.powerHousePackaging.com

Printed by Toppan Leefung

Book design by Robert Avellan

Library of Congress Control Number: 2020930668

ISBN: 978-1-57687-946-7

10 9 8 7 6 5 4 3 2 1

Printed in China